Clifford's puppy days

MW00902981

CHRISTMAS ANGEL

By Quinlan B. Lee
Illustrated by John Kurtz

Based on the Scholastic book series "Clifford The Big Red Dog" by Norman Bridwell.

ISBN 0-439-75533-6

12 11 10 9 8 7 6 5 4 3 2   5 6 7 8 9 10/0

Designed by Michael Massen

Printed in the U.S.A.   First printing, November 2005

SCHOLASTIC INC.

New York   Toronto   London   Auckland   Sydney
Mexico City   New Delhi   Hong Kong   Buenos Aires

When Clifford woke up one winter morning, he was
surprised that Emily Elizabeth was already out of bed.
He went to look for her and got an even bigger surprise.
There was a large tree in the living room!

"Hey, Little Red," Norville called from the windowsill, "what do you think of the tree? It's a beaut, isn't it? The Howards brought it inside because it smells so nice."

Daffodil hopped into the living room. "Oh, Norville," she said, "that's not why the Howards have the tree! The tree is here because Christmas is tomorrow."

What does a tree have to do with Christmas? wondered Clifford.

"Good morning," said Emily Elizabeth. "I woke up
early because I was so excited to see the Christmas tree.
We're having a party tonight to decorate it!"

Clifford barked happily. He still didn't know what a tree had to do with Christmas, but he loved parties!

After breakfast, Clifford helped Emily Elizabeth wrap presents. There were presents for everyone!

The doorbell rang. "Emily Elizabeth, can you please get that?" called Mrs. Howard from the kitchen.
"Sure, Mom," replied Emily Elizabeth.

Flo and Zo had arrived with Mr. Solomon. The cats bounded into the room to play with Clifford . . . but they couldn't find him anywhere.

Then they noticed that one present was wiggling.

The cats tipped the present over. Out came Clifford!
"What were you doing in there?" asked Zo.
"Are you someone's present?" asked Flo.

"I don't think so," Clifford replied. "Why are all these presents here?"

"They're here because it's Christmas," Zo answered.

"Presents are what Christmas is all about," added Flo. Now Clifford was even more confused. Christmas was about trees, parties, *and* presents?

A few hours later, Clifford was amazed at all the changes to the living room. Now there were stockings, wreaths, and twinkling lights. Clifford explored everything.

"Silly puppy!" Emily Elizabeth giggled. "That hat's too big for you. Try this one—it will keep you warm on your walk with Jorgé."

"It sure smells terrific in there," Jorgé said.
"Mr. and Mrs. Howard have been cooking all morning," said Clifford. "They're getting ready for the party tonight."

"The food isn't just for tonight's party,"
said Jorgé. "They're cooking for Christmas tomorrow,
too. The delicious food makes Christmas merry."
The food? Clifford wondered. *What about the presents,
the tree, and the party?* He felt more confused than ever.

Finally it was time for the party! All of the
Howards' friends helped decorate the tree.

Mrs. Howard took an ornament out of a box and showed it to Nina's mom. "Aren't these beautiful?" she said. "They remind me of everything wonderful about Christmas."

Whatever Christmas is must be in that box, thought Clifford. He decided to climb into the box to see for himself.

When Mr. Solomon reached into the box to get another ornament, he pulled out Clifford instead. "What are you doing in there, Clifford?" Mr. Solomon asked. "Someone might think you're a decoration!"

"That's a great idea!" said Mr. Howard. "I know just the place where we can put Clifford so we won't lose him again." He lifted the little red puppy high up and perched him at the top of the tree.

Clifford looked down on the party.
Everyone was smiling.
All his friends and family were
happily celebrating being together.

Emily Elizabeth climbed up and took Clifford down.
"Isn't Christmas wonderful?" she asked.
Clifford gave her a big kiss. This time he knew exactly
what she meant.